Q & U
CALL IT QUITS

Written by Stef Wade

Illustrated by Jorge Martin

Quill Tree Books
An Imprint of HarperCollinsPublishers

Quill Tree Books is an imprint of HarperCollins Publishers.

Library of Congress Control Number: 2020934019
ISBN 978-0-06-297068-8

The artist used Photoshop to create the digital illustrations for this book.

Typography by Rachel Zegar
21 22 23 24 25 RTLO 10 9 8 7 6 5 4 3 2 1
❖
First Edition

To Tom, I'll never QUit you.
—S.W.

To the Ms and Gs in my life
—J.M.

From the first day Q and U met, they were quick friends. Just like T and H, who were thick as thieves, Q and U were a squad.

Q clung to U's side every day. They did crafts.

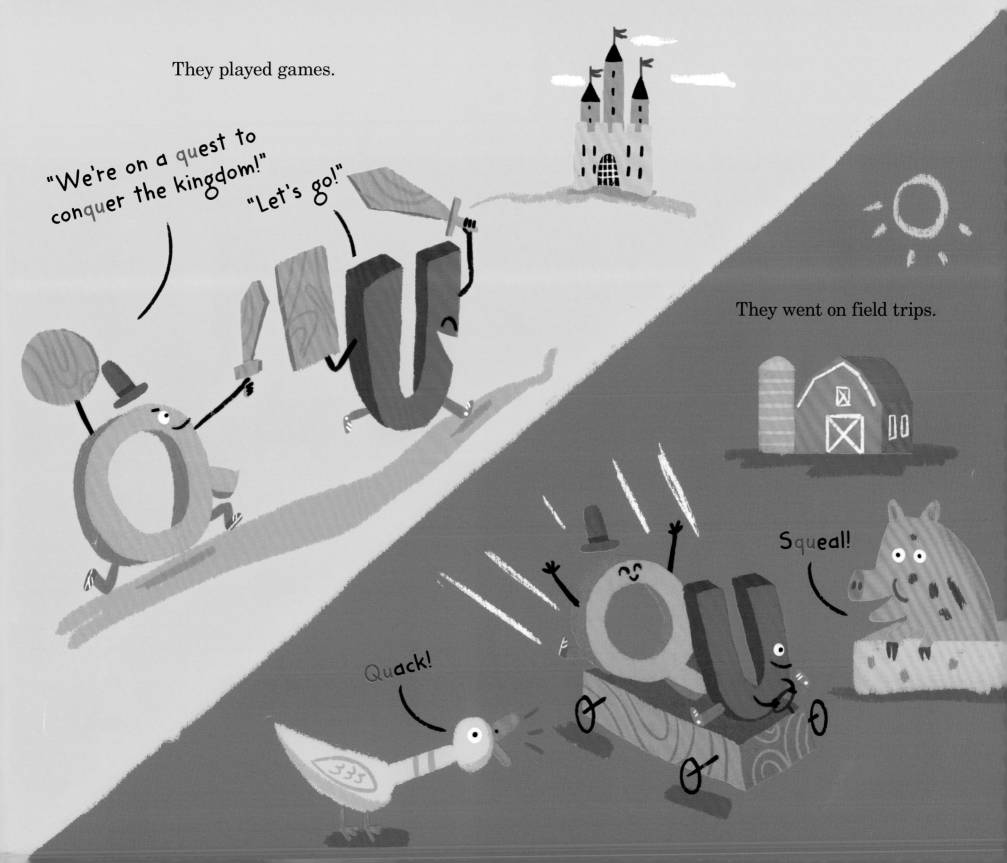

They played games.

"We're on a quest to conquer the kingdom!"

"Let's go!"

They went on field trips.

Quack!

Squeal!

But even though they were good friends, there was a problem. As much as Q loved U, U began to see that Q needed her more than she needed him.

Q felt useless when U tried to fix things with her friend N.

"Never fear!"   "We'll untie it!"

He was lonely when U hung out with her friend S and left him by himself.

"Just the two of us!"

Q tried to branch out and make new friends, but it never quite worked.

"Hey, qids!"

"Nice try, buddy, but I got this.
Hey, kids!"

U could see Q was feeling left out, but she wanted to hang with her other friends, too. Being Q's only friend was exhausting.

One day, U decided she'd had enough. So she told Q she was taking a break to be alone.

"I'm sorry, but I think I need to be unattached for a while."

U went and sat under her umbrella to enjoy some time to herself.

Word of Q and U's split traveled fast. Everyone came together to discuss the news.

"It's hard to always be grouped together."

It wasn't long before everyone wanted some time alone.

So they all split up. . . .

"You're always slowing me down."

"We're just wrong for each other."

One by one, they went off by themselves.

S sang her favorite song.

R ran in a race.

C cooked corn on the cob.

And they were happy.

But pretty soon, everyone's world was upside down. S was singing so loudly that P and L didn't want to get anywhere near her, so no one could sleep or play.

When G couldn't catch up to R, there was no more green grass.

And with C mad at H, there was too much corn and no more cheese.

And nothing makes people yell more than not having cheese.

The more things went wrong,
the more the letters argued.

U looked around at the chaos and realized her peaceful break wasn't so peaceful anymore. It was too loud for U to hear her own thoughts.

With S ignoring H, there was no way to SHHH! or HUSH the crowd.

And no one could do anything about it.

While U enjoyed some of her time alone, she realized that she really missed Q and all the fun they used to have.

She looked over at Q and she knew what had to be done.

They both looked at each other and nodded.

The letters turned and stared at Q and U, who looked quite content. They smiled and said, "We request that you make up. And quickly, please. This is getting out of hand."

And after that day, the letters stuck together because they knew life wasn't quite the same if they didn't.

But every once in a while, they spent a few quiet . . . er, silent . . . minutes to themselves.